Moving On

Poems and Sketches

In friendship,
Eileen Curtis, s.s.a.

Moving On

Poems and Sketches

Eileen Curteis

Ekstasis Editions

Canadian Cataloguing in Publication Data

Curteis, Eileen
    Moving on

    Poems
    ISBN 1-896860-13-3

        I. Title.
    PS8555.U84M68 1997   C811'.54   C97-910238-3
    PR9199.3.C8255M68   1997

Acknowledgement:
Some of these poems and drawings have appeared in the follow-
ing periodicals, journals and newspapers:
*Island Catholic News. Prairie Messenger, Sisters Today, CRC Bulletin
(French and English), Grail, The Ocean Magazine.*

I would like to thank Susan McCaslin and Hannah Main-van der
Kamp for their editorial skills and for encouraging me to publish
these poems.

Published in 1997 by:
Ekstasis Editions Canada Ltd   **Ekstasis Editions**
Box 8474, Main Postal Outlet   Box 571
Victoria, B.C. V8W 3S1   Banff, Alberta T0L 0C0

Moving On: Poems and Sketches has been published with the assis-
tance of a grant from the Canada Council and the Cultural Services
Branch of British Columbia.

For Tom and Lil

Beacons in my life

Contents

Moving On

Poems and Sketches

POWER WOMAN

Crumpled city
go down
into the black void
of your nothingness.
Meet her who must die
the death that women die!

Taste her. Feel her. Know her.
Without water
she sits on fire.
Driven by the fierce wind
of a woman's rage,
she does not howl lightly.

There is a power
in each step she takes,
a power
that could make a wolf
soar like an eagle,
even on the bleakest day.

Born of the Wind,
she flies
with wings
that cannot be tapered!

AUTUMN DESTINY

Frigid
as an iceberg in winter,
I know how it feels
to be the last
of the crushed leaves
in Autumn,
so strong
is this stripping
in me.

Knocked down,
pushed over
by one rude slap
of the wind
after another,
I don't give birth
to the white winged
graceful swan
easily,
but I do give birth!

WAIF GIRL

My heart longs to know you
Mother Earth,
but like soot in the chimney
it is black here
where I live.
Beaten,
squashed down,
kicked like a stone,
I cannot die like this
and live.

"Nor should you"
came the Voice from down under.
"It is your turn
to bounce your ball
high over the earth.
Wrinkled,
dried up
prune of a thing,
you are no longer
the waif girl
in the fields
they ploughed under!"

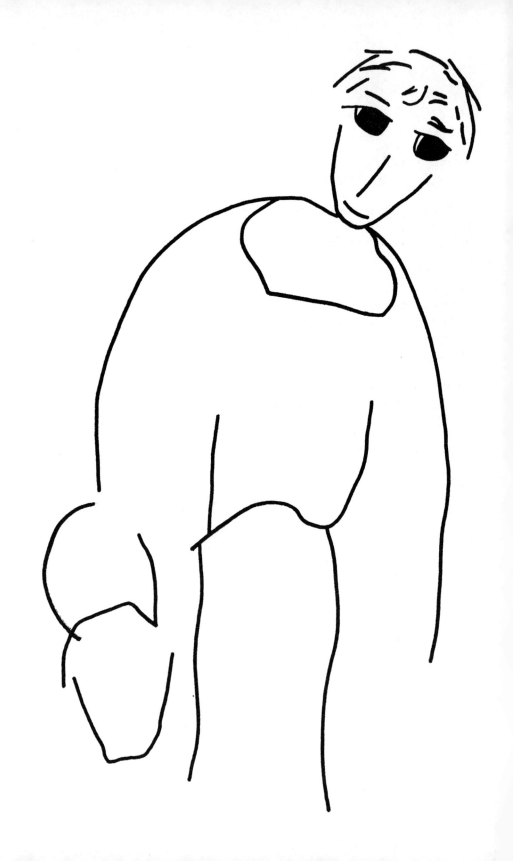

CREAM PAIL

Old one
with the yellow light
in your green eyes
are you the shabby young one
who came hungering for white cream
when there was none?

What became of you
through the years
wild one
purring sweetly
inside the soft skin
of a cat?

Was that torn-off fur
you at the window
or was it just yourself
with the claws
scratched out of you?

RESTORATIVE BOTTLES

Sunflower
stuffed in a shoe,
that's no way
for anyone to grow.

Years ago,
Old Betsy, the school nurse,
told me:
>Shut down
>like piss in a bedpan
>and you'll end up dying
>in your own urine!

You may be small,
city girl,
and urinated on
but it's time
you stopped sipping water
from the spoon
in your dish.

Try the ocean
this time.
It's vaster
than you are
and less stingy!

WINDOW LIGHT

Dark room
filled with the torn face
of a bird
is death as imminent
as I think it is?

If so,
I'll not let dead roots
like black scabs
on a white flower
devour me.
I am too young for that!

Slay me with an axe
and see if I care
which way the knife goes in.
I am alive at forty!

Shut me down
like a closed door
creaking
and I will open wide
my desolate wings.
Newborn at fifty!

Destroy this sky bird
at your window
and in three days
she will live!

OPENING HIDDEN POCKETS

Wanting to speak,
the wooden throat
said to the silent tongue,
"I am too disfigured to look at.

Odd shaped,
my crippled legs
get pulled up
like a wobbly pole
from under me."

"Enough of that talk"
said the caretaker.
"Hidden in purses
or back pockets,
that's no place for you to be.

You're the kind of an animal
that belongs outdoors
blowing free
with your mane in the wind!"

NAKED LAMB

On a desolate beach
where death flapped its wings
for the last time,
I saw love get scooped up
out of the river.
She was anything but mild!

Soft cloud
floating on summer breeze,
I saw not
that side of her.

Instead,
I saw scarred skin
on the hot sands of her feet,
chafed fever red.

Her long hair
tossing in the wind,
she stood there
naked as a lamb
sheared.

REDDEST, RED LEAF

Reddest, red leaf,
I pulled you out of a dead twig
that you might live.

Not that I would crush your bones
anymore than your tiny hands
have tried to do so,
not that I would restrain
your tired feet
from covering new ground
with the moccasins I give you.

Not any of this.

But one thing I ask
reddest, red leaf,
hanging looser than the others
on your tree,
when will you let go
completely?

ROCK WOMAN

Let's be honest,
black cat
sneaking around
with slippers
soft as a pussie's fur,
that's not you at all!

You're in denial
about something.
Throwing rocks
into the basement
you got kicked out of.

Pitching stones
at your own face
in the mirror,
that's more like it
isn't it?

Black cat, get real!

BERRY GIRL

White dress
stained by a purple berry,
I'll not wear you any longer,
nor will I come into your house
lugging myself
like a suitcase I cannot carry.

There will be nothing heavy
in my basket this time,
a little fruit, perhaps,
and a garment less stiff
than the one I wore
in the Fall.

With the soft stone
of an angel,
I'll replace the hardness in me,
and with the soul of a flute
I'll dance out of this old body
into the new one!

PEASANT WOMAN

Fluttering her wings
like a seagull
under the sand,
nobody saw how hard
this peasant girl
tried to live.

Invisible, as an unwanted child,
her sad arms
lay huddled under her.

Cut fingers
scraped out of a cavern,
limp body
dragged over a chisel,
little nomad
did not die
for nothing!

Searching for Love
and finding it,
the heart
is the home
this gypsy
wandered into.

WAKING WOMAN

Dozing child
grew
into a furious spider
dangling
in her no good web.

Perfect woman, she said,
flattened beach ball,
I'll not bounce to your rhythm
any longer!

I'll spit out stored anger
wrapped up like an Egyptian mummy.
I'll tell her:
> Give me flaws anytime
> and I'll sit
> with my wrinkled dress
> all over them,
> comfortable
> in a plain chair
> in a plain room
> on a day as ordinary as this!

MYSTERIOUS STRANGER

In a deserted village
a stranger lived
inside the thin body
of a young owl.

Whenever night came
and the birds molested her
she flew high
into the trees.

Falling into a deep silence
she lay still
in the arms
of a cedar.

Some say
the great Spirit entered her
and like the grandmother
of an old owl
she went about doing good.
Others say they saw nothing
but two dark eyes
in the foliage.

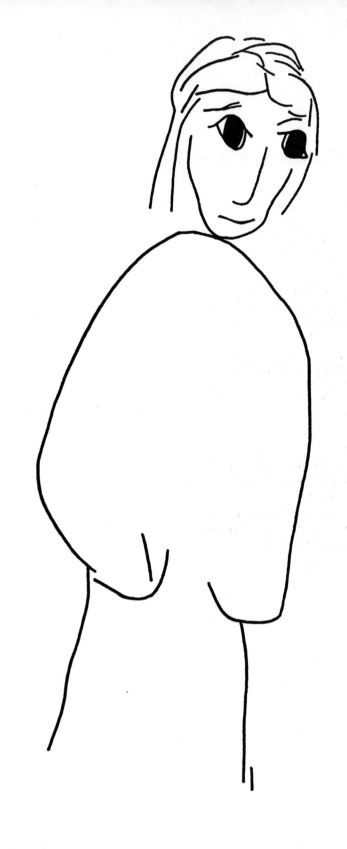

ENLIGHTENED MADONNA PURIFIED

Each night
with pierced eyes
the colour of gold
sun daughter returns home
from her day.

Enlightened one,
shaking dusk
out of dawn,
she flops down
like a ruby
in the dark tunnel
of things.

Seen polishing the floor
of God's kitchen
some say, she's the healer,
waiting to be healed.
Others say, like Jesus,
life chained her to a tree.

Whoever she is
black madonna, white madonna,
like hornets
the thorns pass through her hair.

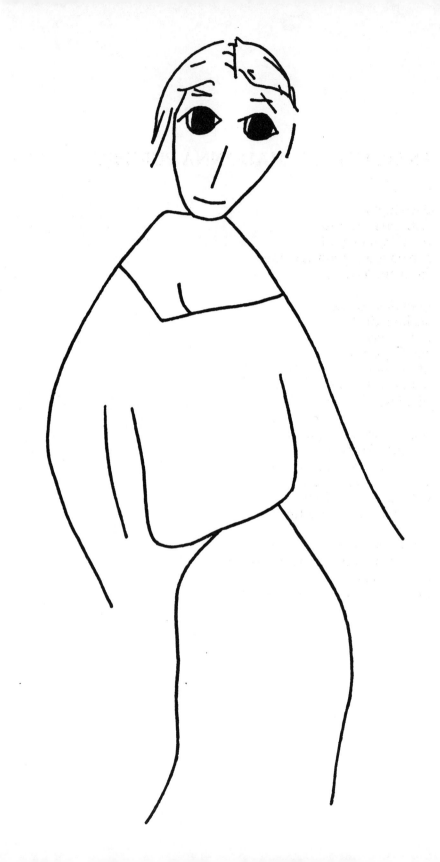

MOVING ON

One day
thrush flew out of the ashes
with bones delicate enough
to make you sing.
It was cinder girl
turning into a woman.

Against her stooped body
she could feel
the frailty
of small wings pushing.

Loosening her matted feathers
there was something more here
than a face
chiselled by the wind.

You could see it
in her eyes,
a Power stronger than steel
and in her voice
a lifetime's journey!

FARM DAUGHTER LEAVING HOME

This skeleton
has the brain of an angel.
Born in the dark cave
of her mother
she cannot return there
nor should she.

A brave soul
with the heart of a scooter
she makes her way out the door
still faltering
with the unsteady steps of a toddler.

In the big world
mistaken for sweet grass
or hay stuffed under the barn
she could be any farm girl
munching on her sadness.

Years later
I can still see her
leaving home
this skeleton
with the brain of an angel.

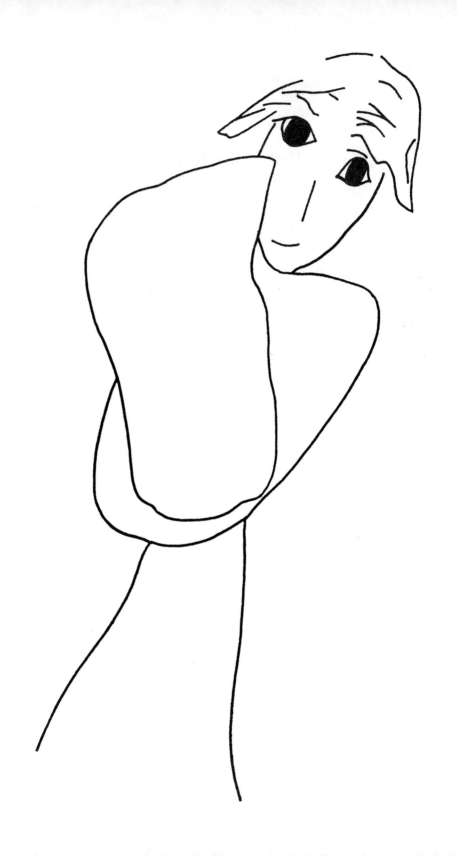

PRECIOUS PARCEL
THE SELF INFUSED WITH LIGHT

Not garbage
but courage
pulled out of a wastebasket
that's the way
my body knows me!

Face it
she says:
You're not the only lonely whistle
on a freight train
dying in its tracks.

Look at yourself.
Nerves shot down
to a pulp.
It's time pain
the irritable black fly
came out of you.

Small parcel of my precious self
if this be death to me
then put a soul in my light bulb
and let me live!

LONELY CLOWN TRANSFORMED

Funny little clown
that I am
turning my face
in the opposite direction
when the stones hit me.

Burying myself
as if the loneliness
of a bulldozer
ploughing me under
didn't matter.

Dying strange deaths
then turning up in the soil
as an illiterate earthworm
you stepped on
I'd like to come out of this school
less of a hunchback
than when I went in.

A baker, maybe,
who gives free buns to the needy
or a genius
who mends clothes for the poor.

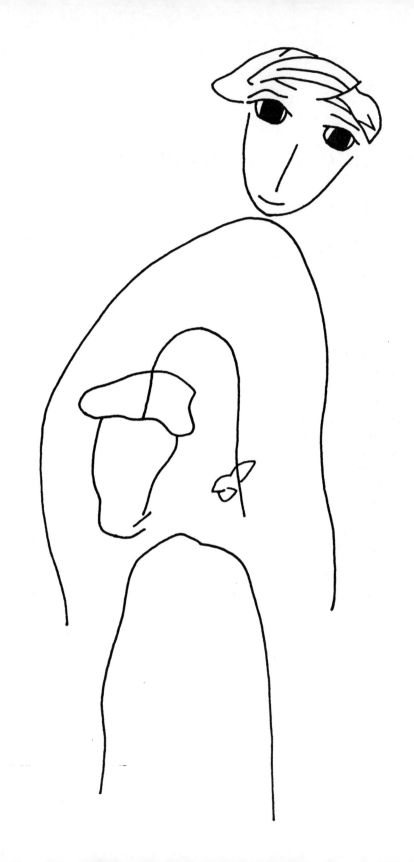

SPRING FLOWERS BLOOMING

Sore feet
tunnelling through the earth
we saw them in the midst of winter
disfigured birds
thousands of them
trudging in the sand.

Flattened, without energy,
the first one fell
into the hands of a surgeon.
Bandaging her wounds
he squeezed hard
on the soft face of flamingo
thinking her human.

Unable to fly
she did not let
death at the roots
mar her.

Silently blooming
I think she saw
spring flowers
in the barren earth
before we did.

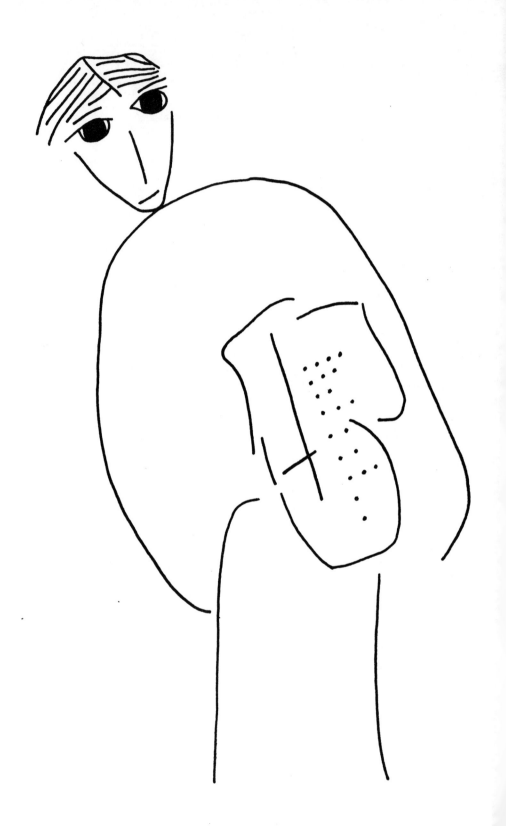

INNER CODE

Sometimes the silent screams
of a small girl bursting
is what you have to kiss yourself
good-bye to.

Sometimes it's the violence
of broken dishes
in a woman's kitchen
that causes her to rage
at the man who slapped her.

Sometimes it's the worn clothes
in a cramped suitcase
you get rid of
that bring you to your senses.

Sometimes there is no warning
the heart clangs
like a siren
and you must love her!

VOICE OF COMPASSION

Cruel
as ships sinking in the sea
we know not the tragedy of another
until our own lives
be lost in this drowning.

ORANGE BUTTERFLY GOES LEAPING

Purple, colour of iris,
thumping its joy into me—
it's happening
something positive
like Spring.

Yes, people of the earth,
I'm celebrating me
small one
with brown boots up to my chin
coming out of the black mud
forever and forever.

See me, now,
an orange butterfly.
Into the blue air called sky
I go leaping.
Beyond the fence,
beyond the wall,
into the blue air called sky
I go leaping.

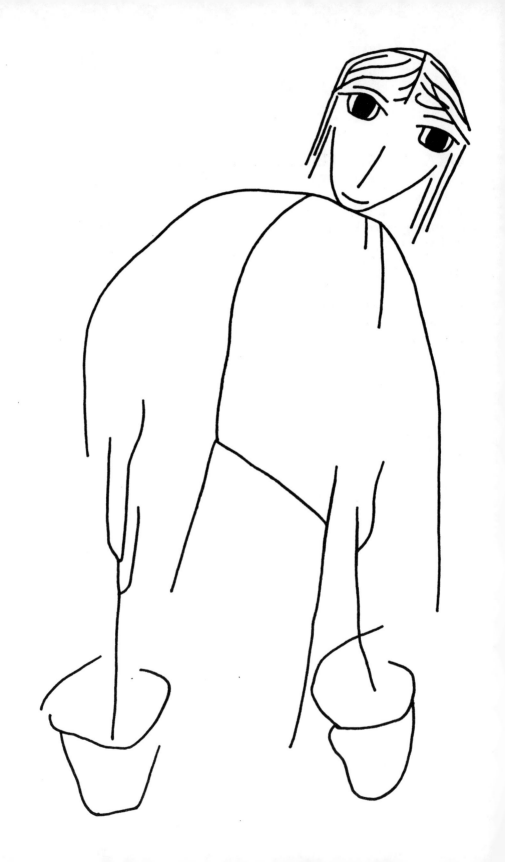

BEYOND THIS DESERT

Swallowing
burnt crumbs from the table
it's hard to imagine
what this kind of sacrifice led to.

But I do remember—
a desert of sweet cakes
cacti
foaming in the mouth
telling me to stop
this stupid kind of denial!

Less indulgent, now,
I've become a whirlwind
blazing in the trees
but I do not catch fire!

A house
suffocated against itself
is no longer
where you'll find me!

WINTER SNOWDROP INTO SPRING

In public
her face glowed with oil of Spring
and we believed her when she said:
>   It's nobody's fault
>   love gets sealed in an envelope
>   it just does.

Dancing
with the foot of a snowdrop
she appeared to us
lighthearted, at first.

Later
we saw her as she was
reckless
as an earthquake in winter.

Tears,
big as the puddles
a child romps in,
she did not let
this grief inhabit her.

Dancing
with the foot of a snowdrop
she appeared to us lighthearted.

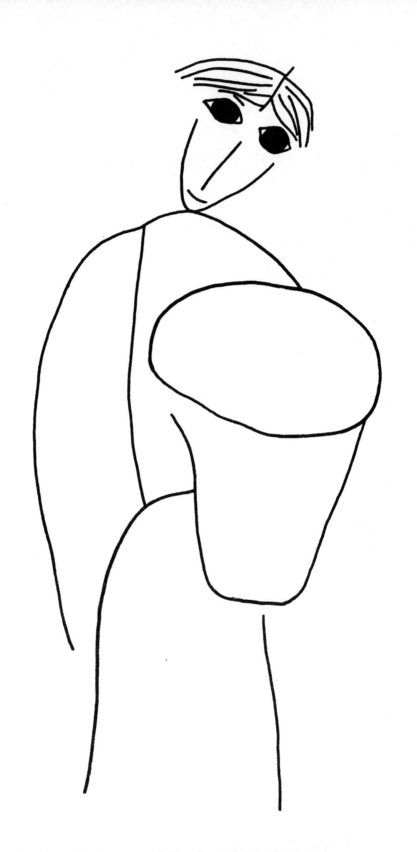

SOLILOQUY
TO THE WORM IN MY BUCKET

Big tear
in a wet handkerchief
slow, slimy
slug of a thing
how much more
can I be drenched by you?

And you,
worm of the earth,
without a hole
to crawl into
where do you live,
how do you grow?

What plans do you have
and is there a future in you?
Is your skin tight
and do you wear a muzzle at night
or are you what I think you are
free of those bodily cares?

Big tear,
little worm in my bucket,
I think I could be like you.

WANDERER IN CAMOUFLAGE

It was January
the month of hibernation
when raccoon
went strutting over the blind earth.

Unimportant
as grey light shining
on a dull evening,
she felt like Mrs. Nobody
going down
in a balloon that bursts its air.

Flat and ragged,
she could have been
the last piece
of anonymity there was.

Fortunately, she bumped into snail,
who said:
Bless me, for I have small feet
and travel slowly.

Bless me, too, said raccoon,
for I wear my mask backwards
not to be seen by anyone
until the time comes.

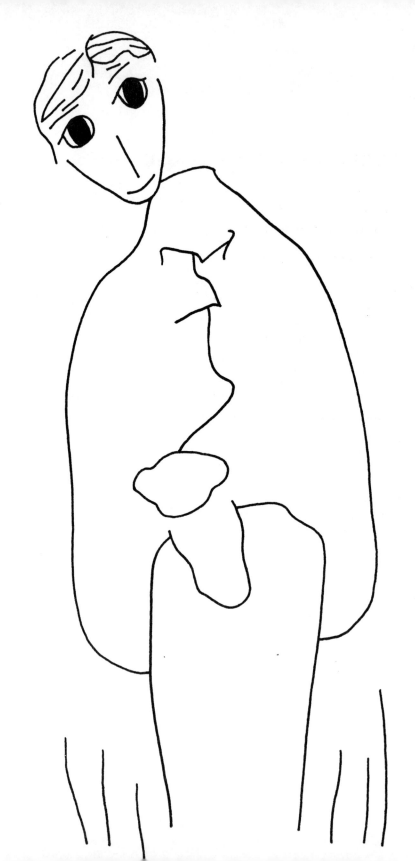

HOW THE GREEN ONE GREW

Many years ago
further back than I can remember
I was in the world waiting to be born
waiting, waiting.

I was hungry for food
real food, the God food.
Nothing came of it
until the great day of the hollow burp
when the vinegar of Jesus passed down through me.

Oh, how I hated the burp,
but God was in the burp and the burp was in God.
Finally, God spoke, and I listened.

Famished one, God said,
swallow your own burp and live.
It will not eat you!
From then on the green one grew.

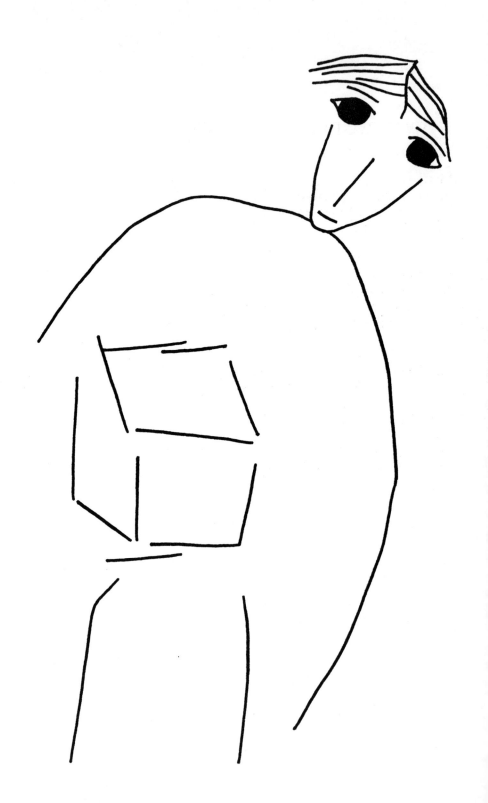

BOX TURTLE REVIVES

Turtle had a voice
and a good one
but one day she closed down
like the lid of a padlock
you couldn't open.

Inside her box, inside her shell,
racehorse had told turtle
not to go running, running, running
in a relay never to be won
but she had not listened.

Wanting to be first
she played the game:
    Hurdle me over
    push me down
    crack my head
    and I'll wear a crown!

Years later,
collapsing like a bed on the floor,
she saw racehorse under the covers
and they became best friends,
world travellers,
hiking into the high zone
of the Unknown Way.

THE DESERTED TOWN
I MOVE BEYOND

Always you come
like foxes in the night
knocking on the door
of my den.

What is it you want
that I have not already given,
food, home, clothing,
you have eaten all my possessions
and still you come for more?

There is no more!
Just me
black ghost
flaring up my chimney!

Swirling into a cloud
I could be victorious
as a white flag flying in the wind
were not your love
such a betrayal.

Treacherous, as memory is,
I will not be seen
dragging my coffin
into a town that has deserted me!

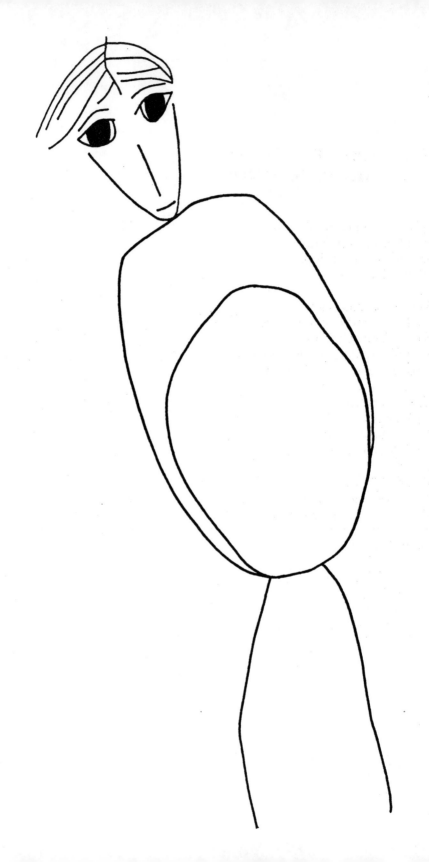

THE BOULDER WILL SET YOU FREE

Skidding, over the jagged ice in winter,
I went on the tributary of this misshapen river
to do my own rowing.
Rudderless, and without oars,
I thought I fell into the helm of God steering.
Instead of that, I slid down
the wrong side of a skinny old cliff, crying–
Is that you, God, gouging my face out of a boulder?

No, came the answer.
The gully is you
falling into it.
Learn to love yourself
by loving your enemy the tiger.

Own it,
she's the dark shadow
in your troubled body–
    angry bear, jealous moose,
    sad monkey, guilty grizzly,
    fearful chipmunk,
she's all part of the same person
called you.

Love her
as the only boulder worth holding!

BLADE OF GRASS QUIETLY ASSERTIVE

Sure
as a four-footed dog
goes yapping down the alley
it wouldn't be my form of survival!

I suppose I could get your attention
by raising my voice or barking loudly
but, truly, I'd be happier
lying quietly on a blade of grass
content not to have
the rackety sound of a tractor
running its noise over me.

I know what you're thinking,
passive old woman
in a rickety rocker,
but that's not me at all!

I actually like being assertive
showing up in places
where the wrinkles are
and scooping the cobwebs out of them.

And, yet, there's a quieter me
who goes home
kissing the warts of another
and puts herself to bed.

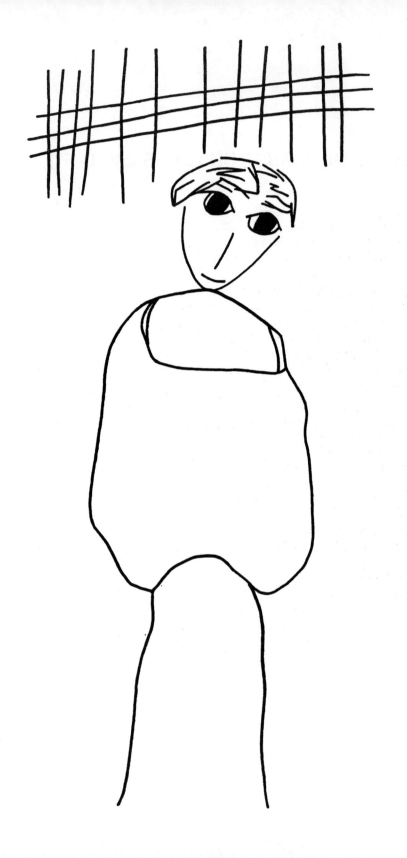

WHITE LIGHT BEHIND THE FENCE

A woman waits for you.
She waits and waits.
A cold wind from the inside
blows heavily on her.
To all appearances
she has the pained look of a foreigner
but she is not a foreigner.

Tight coat
veiled eyes
she could be anybody's visitor
walking past you
and you would not miss her.

Living in a high tower,
she's the walled in one
whose face is the fence
you cannot get through.

Longing for intimacy,
she's the white light
after the thick fog
leaves you.

DOOR OPENER

Fury, black stain on my towel,
how dare you do this to me
how dare you say
my face is washed
my skin is clean
when the suds on my toes know otherwise.

I've seen fury
grow like an iron
over my burnt clothes,
and I've said,
wardrobes are the false garments that we wear
the don't-touch-me categories
of our hundred thousand different faces.

And worse than that
fury is my best friend turning her face on me
with the pointed spike of a porcupine
distancing herself in a game called love.

Go home, fury, and rest awhile
there are other worlds out there...
put a scorched match
under your door
and let the air come in!

TULIP, YODELLING THE NEW YEAR IN

Tulip,
at the foot of my garden,
if a hose could sponge me down
I'd turn out differently this time.

Less private
and more open,
I'd put up a sign:
   Faucet in the trees
   oddities welcome!

Floating in on a barge,
I'd be a Persian cat
with big ears
the size of an elephant,
saying, look at me now,
clean as a tub to bathe in.

Unharmed,
by the booing of a crowd,
I'd stand there
with my lungs open
yodelling
the New Year in!

A GOOD SOUL

Skirts, tangled in the wind,
this dog sniffs me
improperly,
pushes his nose
up my fanny,
and licks the salt
off my skin.

Shocking, isn't it,
the things animals do,
mimicking people
who cut you off
from the hip down
as if you had something lacking.

Good girls
don't go public
but I'm not a good girl.
Only my soul is!

LIGHTHOUSE SHINING IN THE SEA

In burdensome weather,
you don't put out
the glimmer of a lighthouse
shovelled under the sea,
nor do you go
rough trod over her.

Treating her badly
she'll turn up elsewhere,
a discarded candle, maybe,
with the eyes
of a night light
you cannot extinguish!

Feeling sorry for herself,
she's not the type
to be bathing her feet
over a bruised rock
when the foundation
has been taken from under her.

In good weather
or bad,
she will shine
no matter what!

WHITE DOVE IN THE KILN

A love
passionate enough
to change the world,
it could have been my own hand
fingering the face of Jesus
the night after He died.

Not likely though.
History turned backwards
doesn't work that way.

Even the good Book says—
    Put Jesus on a sofa
    and you're lying on the wrong bed.
So much for the easy route.

Picture instead
a woman with clay feet
tough as a cougar
pawing the belly of God open!

With pure eyes
she sees, now,
the dandruff in her,
white dove in a kiln
fluttering vigorously!

COMPASS MOVER

Compass
screwed into a wall,
I can't pretend to know
where I'm going,
but I'm going!

Strapped down
like a suspender,
I'll pull up my own trousers,
thank you,
and be on my way!

Small girl
with a crooked smile,
I'll be out there
blooming like a dimple
when the time comes.

If tragedy be my teacher,
I'll pick her up
like a baby in a carriage,
cradling my own injury
if you please.

Choosing life,
I'll put joy in the mouth of a dragon,
and tell her she belongs to me!

THE GLORY OF BEING RAKED UNDER

Measles, grubs, scabs,
come Spring
we'll all be raked under,
little mud pies
shovelled under the earth.

Words, phrases, speeches,
no amount of eloquence
can bring us back to life,
not even nature
with its bugs
running ecstatically over us.

What we need
is rapture,
delicious
as a piece of Mozart
to get us through our day!

FIRE DANCE

Spinning
like a wheel
off its axle,
could be
God rolling down a hill
and we just don't see her.

Invisible as she is,
God could be driving past us
on the highway
wearing the skin of a zebra,
and we still don't see her.

Mysterious God,
red flame
burning like a bonfire,
how obvious does love have to be
before the lightning strikes?

Evasive woman,
dancing in the fire,
could be
God in the furnace
with us!

FIERCE LOVE

From the beginning
Love laces her boots
backwards.
She learns early
misfits
like old shoes
get tramped over,
left behind.
Still, Love remains
tied into them.

Wherever Love goes
Love dreams
of getting out of the callous
she puts her foot into.

One day,
Love grows wings
big as eagle's.

From now on Love knows
burnt green
is the colour of an old weed
choking the earth,
the colour of her first self
she wants to get rid of,
and so Love does!

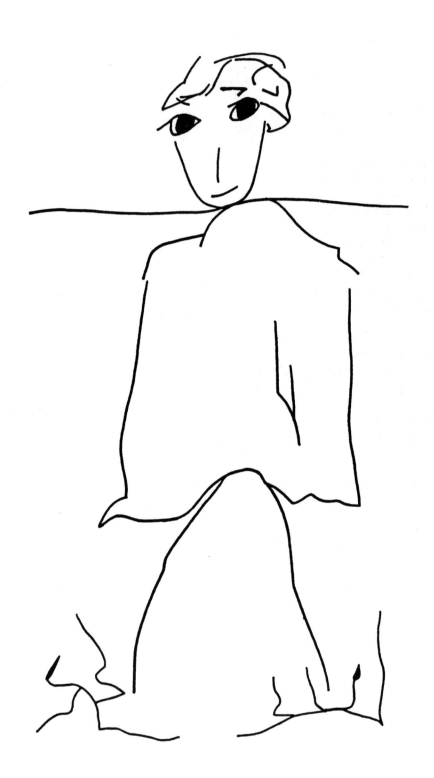

STARCHED OUT
SOFT AND LUMINOUS AS THE MOON

Starched fingers,
I am the knotted one
with a soft comb
in my tangled hair,
the tight one
with the stiffened dress
all around her.

Hidden in a cluttered room
I sit quietly,
unwinding myself like a yoyo.
Nobody can loosen
my threads
the way I can.

Hard layers
peeled off
the skin of an onion,
face of rag woman
coming toward me,
my face
grown soft
and luminous as the moon!

Printed in April 1997 by

in Boucherville, Quebec